I0623414

OZONI AND ONSENS

MISO COZY MYSTERIES
BOOK 3

STEPH GENNARO

ONIGIRI PRESS

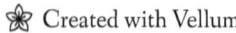

OZONI AND ONSENS

This book is dedicated to tangy, delicious seaweed. Yum.

———

FOREWORD

This book is an interstitial story between *The Daydreamer Detective Braves the Winter* and *The Daydreamer Detective Opens a Tea Shop*. It is not a traditional mystery.

———

In Japanese, the most common way of showing respect to another person's social standing is with the use of honorific suffixes that are appended on the end of either first or last names. The most common, -san, means either Mr., Ms., or Mrs.

In earlier versions of this book, and in the whole series, I did use these honorific suffixes. But for 2019 and onward, I have switched to the English way in order to make this series more accessible to English speakers. I hope you enjoy this version!

The town in this novel, Chikata, is completely fictional, though the area I put it in is not. Saitama prefecture is located to the west of Tokyo, and many of the eastern areas are considered to be suburbs of the city. Chikata is located farther out west, nearer to the prefectures of Nagano and Gunma.

CHAPTER
ONE

I double checked my bag — an extra sweater, underwear, fuzzy socks, and disposable heating pads for long, cold, romantic walks outside. I was sure I had everything, but I consulted my list one more time, just in case.

"I know you deserve this vacation, but I wish you'd be here tomorrow morning. We've never spent a New Year's Day apart before," Mom said, wringing her hands, her forehead scrunched with worry. She wasn't trying to make me feel guilty, not really. She was just concerned for the future if we didn't spend the most auspicious day of the year together.

"I get it, Mom, but Yasahiro planned this trip. He didn't even want me involved, wanted to plan the whole thing himself. I think he's spent so many New Year's days apart from his family it doesn't faze him. I'd like to be a little more flexible, if I can." I set my hand on each stack of clothes in my bag, mentally counting the clothing.

"You're right, you're right. I'll try not to worry." But even as she said it, her voice sounded more worried than ever. My mom was superstitious, and we had always spent New Year's Day together as a family because she believed that would keep us together forever. My brother, his wife, and kids also came to eat *ozoni* soup and have special box lunches around the kotatsu. Spending the day with my boyfriend was out of the normal.

Though I promised myself I wouldn't feel guilty for taking some downtime, my familial duties weighed on me like a sumo wrestler crushing his opponent. Deep down inside, it felt wrong, but I wanted to give it a shot. There wasn't a better time for Yasahiro to take off work. This was it. After the new year, we had a lot of tasks to do on the tea shop and at Sawayaka. We both needed a vacation.

I wheeled my bag into the main room of the house, stopping to turn on the space heater, grateful Mom had enough money to be here a few times per week. Though I was living out of Yasahiro's apartment most days, the majority of my belongings were at the house. Yasahiro dropped me off to pack at seven and said he would be back by eight to get me with coffee and pastries.

I followed Mom into the kitchen where she was already preparing food for tomorrow. It would be a sparse but tasty meal since Mom was trying to make every yen count. My sister-in-law volunteered to bring sweets, her favorite thing to prepare, and for once Mom hadn't made a fuss over it. I was sure they'd have a brilliant day, and my heart squeezed knowing I wouldn't be there.

You deserve time off, Mei.

"Will you see Chiyo and everyone at the temple tomorrow morning?" I asked, tightening my sweater around my chest.

"We'll meet here after sunrise, around seven. Then we'll all go out to pray at the temple and come back for soup and oranges." Every New Year's Day, Mom prepared our family's ozoni soup for everyone. It was something she knew by heart and could put together at a moment's notice. My mouth watered, imagining what I would miss, but I'd hear all the stories on January third.

A car door slam echoed through the front room before the door opened. "I'm back!" Yasahiro called out. "It looks like you're packed."

He entered the kitchen with three cups of coffee in a carrier and a pastry box wrapped with twine. Mom's face broadened with a smile. She had a soft spot for pastries. Yasahiro knew how to stay on her good side. He was better at it than I was, which would come as no great shock to anyone.

"So, are you ready for three days worth of relaxation? I've been dying to go to this hotel forever, and since my friend became head chef there, I've owed him a visit for too long."

I ate half my chocolate croissant and sipped my coffee in one go. "I'm definitely ready for relaxation. I feel like I've been running at a hundred kilometers per hour for months on end. This trip is needed indeed."

I glanced at Mom who was enjoying her pastry, and I was relieved to see her nod her head. "You've been working hard, Mei. I hope you both enjoy your trip. I'll say extra prayers for you at the temple tomorrow." This was probably the best Mom could do under these circumstances. I would take all the extra prayers I could get.

Yasahiro looked between the two of us before clearing his throat and grabbing his coffee. "Shall we get on the road? I don't know how much traffic we'll hit on the way to Hakone."

We grabbed my bag, and saying goodbye to Mom at the front door, we hugged and bowed goodbye. Yasahiro hefted my bag into the trunk, and I waited for him in the car, watching Mom through the front windshield. She looked smaller and older when I was away from her, and my breath caught in my throat.

Yasahiro slid in and turned up the heat, waving to Mom as he pulled out of the driveway. "Your mom seems worried. Is everything okay?"

"She's fine. Just concerned about spending New Year's Day apart. I told her not to be so superstitious, that we'd be fine."

"I see. Let's bring something back for her and call her tomorrow."

I turned in my seat to look at the house as we approached the road. Mom was still there, watching us go. I waved my hand for one last goodbye, but I couldn't be sure she saw me.

You need a break, Mei.

I just needed to say it a few more times to believe it.

CHAPTER
TWO

I was on vacation.

I needed to let that sink in for a moment. I hadn't been on vacation in, well, over five years, and boy did I deserve it. When I had graduated from college, Mom took me to Sapporo and Hokkaido for five days. We'd traveled there in April and the land was still covered by a meter's worth of snow. It was a beautiful trip, but it wasn't much of a vacation. It was my same life moved to a different part of the country, with Mom and her food and every bit of emotional baggage we treasured. And I was a summer girl. I really loved the summer. I would've preferred to have gone to Okinawa, but Mom wanted to go to Sapporo, and she was paying, not me.

But this wasn't a trip with my mom. I was going on vacation with Yasahiro. Nothing could beat a romantic getaway with a brand-new boyfriend even if the weather was bristling cold. It would only be three days — New Year's Eve today, New Year's Day tomorrow, and then drive home on January 2nd — but I would make them count.

Yasahiro slowed the car as he pulled off the highway and

into Hakone. Hakone was a town to the south of Mount Fuji and well-known for being a hot springs resort. The French architecture of the town rolled along the hills, and steam gushed from the stacks on top of buildings housing hot springs. The late morning light bounced off the melted snow and blinded me, and my heart buzzed with excitement. Hakone was a closer drive than Beppu (another popular hot spring resort town), and Yasahiro had ties here, so it made the perfect holiday spot.

"Oh wow," he said, leaning forward over the dashboard to look out the windshield. "This place hasn't changed much in ten years."

"Is that how long it's been since you were here last?" I pulled my phone out of my bag and checked the map. "I came here with friends when I was in college. We only stayed a day and night but we had a great time." Thinking back on my trip, I remembered how Akiko diligently researched the onsens. She'd called five different hotels before finding one that would suit us, and everyone had been so kind. It'd been a stark contrast to the trips of my youth when I was recovering from my burn scars.

"You're suddenly very quiet," Yasahiro said, turning down a side street. He glanced over at me, and I could feel his concern across the car. "What's wrong?"

I turned off my phone and chucked it into my bag. "Nothing. Just reminiscing."

He looked to the side at me, but I looked out the window. We were only a few blocks from our hotel, and maybe, if I prayed enough, things would go well. I had forgotten to vet the hotels Yasahiro showed me before coming here. I thought, for once, I'd let a boyfriend handle the plans instead of me micromanaging every little thing. There were days when I felt like a whole, unscarred person, especially when I was in love and someone else loved me back, despite my flaws. I felt normal, even though I looked far from it.

Change the subject.

I took a deep breath and let it all out, my favorite way to release tension without looking like I needed it. I had made it through another stressful murder investigation, my second one in as many months, while Yasahiro was in Paris, and we had just spent several days apart, him working hard at the restaurant and me helping Mom defrost things at home. We'd all moved out of the house — me, Mom, and Mimoji — during the severe cold of early December, and even though the outlook was for frigid days in January, Mom had finally received paychecks and could afford heat. The temperatures had warmed up, and she was able to defrost the pipes. She told me not to move home until spring, though, and I suspected she was looking out for my relationship with Yasahiro. She also didn't want to see our courtship come to a grinding halt so quickly.

The imposing and formal front of the inn loomed over us as we drove up the driveway, and my hands shook. But if I could handle two murder investigations and a freezing winter, I could handle whatever would come next.

"So, tell me. Why didn't we stay at your friend's hotel?" I asked, as he pulled the car in front and turned into the parking lot.

Yasahiro laughed. "I had two choices. We could either stay at Yoshitomo, which my friends own, or come here. I have another friend here who's the head chef. Since Yoshitomo was booked, I chose this place. Plus I haven't seen Henri in a long time."

Yasahiro parked in one of the guest parking spots and turned off the car. "Besides, this is supposed to be one of the better onsens in town."

Remember, Mei, you're on vacation.

Even if I was apprehensive about being around new people, I could still relax and have a good time. Besides, these were Yasahiro's friends. He'd met plenty of my friends, and it was time for me to do the same for him.

The inn's proprietress met us at the door, bowing and bidding us welcome in a winter kimono. We took off our shoes and left them in the front hall, stepping into the house slippers lined up along the entrance, and a bellhop led us to our room. As I had suspected, Yasahiro had smoothed everything out ahead of time.

The bellhop began a tour of our room while the proprietress set out tea. She knelt at a lovely, dark wood, low table in the center of the room, laid out with snacks, a teapot and cups, and travel brochures about the local sights. I sat with her, and she poured tea.

"Mr. Suga, I'm honored you would choose my inn for a vacation. I've heard many amazing things about your restaurant from Henri and researched it online. It's nice to see people reviving traditional values, especially in our food."

Yasahiro glanced at me, and I could tell he was trying not to roll his eyes. He enjoyed the compliments, but he wanted to be an everyday guy. He was the type of person who struggled with his success, never really believing it. So, compliments like this made him uncomfortable, even if they were genuine.

"Thank you so much for having us on such short notice. I realize your inn is crowded during the holiday season. I'm glad you had a room left for us."

I sipped tea to cover up my smile. Yasahiro was good at all the pleasantries.

"We were lucky to have a cancellation, and I know you're great friends with Henri. We're happy to have you." The woman topped up our tea mugs and stood up. "I invite you both to enjoy the public baths before lunch. Later, while you eat this evening, we will prepare the bath in your private bathroom for you. I'll return in a moment with your *yukata* robes." She bowed as she left the room.

"Mmmm, I'm looking forward to a soak before *and* after dinner," Yasahiro said, raising his eyebrows at me. Our relationship was new enough for me to warm with a blush, knowing what was ahead tonight. We had slept together a dozen times in the past couple of weeks, but it hadn't lost the excitement of a brand-new relationship, with many things to learn about each other.

"Shall we go for a soak and then a walk in the gardens?" He leaned forward to look out at the snow-covered grounds.

"I think I've had enough of snow for now. We must come back in the spring when it's warmer, and we can enjoy a green garden. Let's have a soak and then go shopping after lunch instead." New Year's gifts needed to be purchased!

The door opened with a soft knock. The proprietress had returned, her duties not yet complete.

"I have fresh yukata for you to wear, and I've confirmed you're set for lunch in an hour and dinner at 18:00." She bowed and left again without another word. I liked her. She was kind and polite but unassuming. This was the way I wanted to be when I finally opened my tea shop. After the new year, Yasahiro and I would start our business plans and renovations of his downstairs retail space for my new elderly meeting center and tea shop. Plus, it would be a bento box outpost for Sawayaka, Yasahiro's restaurant.

"Good." Yasahiro rose from his seat and handed me a robe. "Let's get dressed in these and go. My back aches from being in the car for so long." He leaned in and kissed my neck. "I can't wait to get in bed with you later," he whispered in my ear, and my heart raced. I was already looking forward to it.

CHAPTER
THREE

walked into the ladies' dressing room and headed towards the back corner without a care in the world. This would be the start of a great vacation, and I would do it soaking in a nice, hot bath. I found an unoccupied wooden locker, tucked away in the corner, the perfect place for me to hide until I was ready. I sat on the bench and looked into the elegantly furnished and sparkling clean washroom. I couldn't wait to get in there. I took a deep breath and disrobed, placing the yukata in the locker and turning my back to it. The rest of the locker room was empty. Maybe I'd get lucky and there'd be no one around?

Nope. I definitely couldn't be that lucky.

When would I understand that I was an inherently unlucky person?

I grabbed a fresh washcloth at the entrance to the washroom. Several women in a group were already sitting and washing up before going into the baths. They seemed to know each other, laughing and telling jokes while slapping each other on the shoulders and calling to other people outside.

There was no place for me to go except for the station nearest the door, and no one noticed me coming in, so I sat and got to work. This was always my favorite part of bathing at Kumi's bath-house. I loved to scrub up until my skin was pink, then soak in the hot water until I was a lump. Thinking about Kumi, I wished she and Goro had come with us. We talked about making this a double date, me and Yasahiro, Kumi and Goro. But Goro couldn't get away from work. Oh well. I had wanted to spend the holiday alone with Yasahiro, anyway.

I worked up a lather on the washcloth and soaped up both of my arms and shoulders while lost in thought about how I would renovate the retail space in Yasahiro's building. Yasahiro and I had been talking about our budget and who to borrow money from the last two weeks. He planned to donate money and so would Chiyo. Plus, I had money from Hisashi, the money Etsuko had made before she was killed. It wasn't a lot of capital, but it was enough to get me started. I was considering buying used furniture and making a few pieces of furniture myself from recy-cled materials. I had grand plans for a comfortable meeting space, tea and bento boxes, my paintings up on the wall, and a studio space near the back where I could paint. A smile grew on my face just daydreaming about it.

And that was when I realized the room had grown quiet. I looked up and found most of the women gone and in the baths, but two women were present, and they were both watching me.

I bowed to them, smiled, and said, "Good morning," before minding my own business again. I still needed to douse my head in hot water and rinse off before I could move out into the baths, so I refilled the bucket next to my station with hot water. I got lost again in my own daydreams, more comfortable in my head than I was in my body. In my daydreams, I was always a whole person, never scarred, never damaged. It was a safe place for me to be.

When I finished washing, I moved outside and found an

unoccupied corner. The ladies in the baths were quiet, most of them sitting with their eyes closed, and several other women left when I entered, making the scene even more tranquil. I imagined what it would be like to have a place like this at home. Most Japanese bathrooms had a deep tub, but they were nothing compared to this. I loved the extra large tub at Yasahiro's apartment. It fit us both comfortably, and we'd spent many a night together in there in the last week. I closed my eyes and smiled, remembering the holidays and the previous few weeks since he'd returned from Paris.

"Excuse me, Mei," a voice jolted me out of my daydream. "Yes, Mei. You need to come with me." The proprietress in her kimono and wooden sandals bowed from outside the baths. "There's an urgent matter I need you to deal with."

"Is it an emergency? I just got in."

I glanced around and saw I was the only person in the bath. Had I fallen asleep? Everyone had left so quietly.

"Yes, I'm afraid so. You must come deal with this issue at once."

Maybe something had happened to Yasahiro? My heart beat so fast I heard it in my ears. Here I was worried about myself, and I hadn't thought of anyone else. "Is Yasahiro all right?"

The woman averted her eyes as I stepped out of the bath and used the small washcloth to cover my private parts. She glanced at my back and gasped.

"It's okay," I said to her, wrapping my arm over my breasts. "They're just burn scars. I was unlucky as a child."

Her face froze in a frown, and she turned on her heel and marched into the ladies' room. I grabbed a towel, dried off, and got dressed in my robe, all under the watchful eye of the proprietress. She said nothing, despite my earlier questions, and dread grew in my belly like springtime weeds.

I followed her out of the dressing room, and she pointed to a bench in the waiting area. "Wait here, please."

Nervousness fluttered in my stomach. What was going on? Had something happened to Yasahiro? I leaned forward to look out the front door, hoping to God I didn't see an ambulance. The last thing I needed right now was more drama from the police. I'd had just about enough of that, thank you very much.

The men's room door swung open, Yasahiro walked out, ducking under the curtains, and I sank into a pile of relief. He did as well, glad to see me.

"Thank goodness," he said, sighing and grabbing for my hands. "They told me it was an emergency, and I had to come out right away. I thought something had happened to you."

"I thought the same thing." I stopped talking, pressing my lips together, as the proprietress approached us from her office. Her face sported a stern frown, and my gut twisted with fear.

Oh no. I flashed back to my childhood and being bullied by people who didn't care about my feelings. But we were adults now, right?

"I apologize," she said, bowing to us both, "but I'm afraid we must ask you to leave. It's regrettable, but I'll have someone from our staff help you get ready to go."

Yasahiro's mouth fell open, and he looked between me and the proprietress. "What happened?"

"I... I don't know."

The proprietress stared at me, and I felt the blood in my head drain into my torso as I pulled Yasahiro to me.

"You need to leave. I'm sorry. It's very regrettable," she repeated, and when she wouldn't elaborate, dread grew in the pit of my stomach.

"You know what? It's okay," I whispered at him. "We shouldn't make a scene."

"Yes, please," she said, her head still bowed. "If you don't make a scene, we'll be happy to refund you for the entire amount of your stay."

Yasahiro shook his head and closed his eyes. "Wait, wait, wait." He waved his hands in front of his face and pushed away from me. "What happened? We only arrived forty-five minutes ago!" He turned to me, giving the proprietress the cold shoulder. "Did something happen in the baths?"

"No. Nothing happened. I undressed, washed, and I got in the bath with no issues." My body heated from my toes straight up to my face. Yasahiro watched my cheeks brighten, and his lips pinched. This was not a look I understood yet. Was he angry with me? Was he upset? I couldn't tell.

"I see." He clipped the statement short, and I closed my eyes, preparing for the inevitable. One of two things could happen. Either he was annoyed with me for being damaged and ruining his holiday. Or he would yell at the woman. Neither of these two options would be good for me.

"Mei," he whispered, his hand on my upper arm, "please have a seat." He squeezed my hand and had me sit down on the bench.

My heart picked up pace again. What was he going to do? No words had been spoken on the topic of what we did wrong or why. It was unlikely the woman would say anything directly, as this was the way of things in Japan. If Yasahiro did something rash, we might be kicked out of town.

"What are you...?" I started to ask but halted at the firm shake of his head.

"Just wait right here, okay? We'll leave soon." He turned and pointed at the proprietress. "You, come with me."

My body cooled at the sound of his voice. Yasahiro was not someone who bossed around other people. He had a quiet and gentle nature, the kind of person who merely had to smile and ask nicely to get the things he wanted or needed. Even when he was in his busy kitchen, he never raised his voice. This behavior was unprecedented. He had been annoyed with me in the past when I tried to hide that Mom and I were broke and couldn't afford heat, but he was never maliciously angry. The woman's eyes widened, and she followed him around the front desk and down the hallway.

Where were they going?

He told me to stay put, to sit and wait, but my heart urged me to follow. I had only met Yasahiro a few months ago, and in that time, I had gotten to know him in various circumstances. I wanted to see how he would handle this. Because this was only the first time something like this would happen to us, and I was sure it wouldn't be the last.

I peeked around the corner and saw a door swing closed. With the smells of rice cooking and pans clanking emanating from the doorway, it was obvious he had taken the proprietress into the kitchen. I crept up to the door and turned my ear to it.

"Henri, I'm sorry, but I'm afraid we won't be able to have dinner tonight." Yasahiro's voice was sincere and warm. "In fact, we won't be staying here over the holiday."

There was a pause and an abrupt silence as the sounds of cooking stopped.

"What happened? Was something wrong with the room?"

"No. Not at all. The hotel is beautiful, and we were excited to stay here, but it turns out we're not welcome. I hope you'll come visit us in Chikata. I know a woman in town who runs a lovely guesthouse."

There was a longer pause here, and I was tempted to rise to my tiptoes and look through the small window in the door. What were they doing? Just staring at each other?

"I don't know what to say," Henri said, his voice stern. "You're not welcome here? How can that be? You're my guests."

"You'll have to discuss this with your boss." Yasahiro's voice changed, becoming more steely toned and rigid. "And that, madam, is how you will lose business. Putting your guests first should be your utmost priority."

The proprietress echoed Yasahiro's icy tone. "Your girlfriend scared all of my other guests, and she sullied my waters with her disgusting body. If anyone is at fault here, it's you."

I sucked in a quick breath and pressed my lips together to stop a flood of tears. So it *was* me and my burn scars. Why? Why did it always have to be this way?

"Your lack of compassion for someone who has already been through a very traumatic experience is sickening. You should be ashamed of yourself."

Yasahiro's words were just registering in my brain as the door to the kitchen burst open. It startled me so badly I yelped and jumped away, turning to run back down the hallway.

"Mei," he said, grabbing for my arm. "I told you to wait back at the bench."

"You're not the boss of me." A flood of images doused my brain. I saw us vacationing at a beach resort, him in the water and me covered up on a beach chair. I saw us attending swanky restaurant events, other women in sexy backless dresses and me in a dowdy frock. My imagination doomed us. This would never work. I don't know why I always tried to convince myself it would work, but this incident was just the beginning. "I'm leaving. I'll figure out a way to get home."

I stomped off toward our room, and Yasahiro followed me all the way there. He closed the door while I threw off the bathrobe and bent over my bag, naked and looking for something to wear.

Yasahiro came over and stood next to me. "Are you leaving me?" His voice was soft and broke on the last word.

I sighed and didn't look at him as I pulled on a pair of underwear. "This is just the beginning, you know. Just the beginning of ignorant, awful people keeping you from vacations, big events, and making fun of you in the tabloids for dating someone like me. Is this really something you want to deal with for the rest of your life? Because I can tell you it hurts. It hurts a lot. And there's no reason you should be subjected to this too. It's for your own good." I pulled on a shirt and reached for pair of pants, but his hand came down on mine.

"Wait. We're not going to let the actions of some stupid woman tear us apart so easily. Nor will I let all that other stuff bother me either. We're a team." He squeezed my hand. "I *want* us to be a team. The only time I ever want you to break up with me is because I did something wrong, not to save me from you for a ridiculous reason. You need to understand that their opinions mean nothing to me."

"Are you so sure about that? Because I'm sure..." I stopped and cleared my aching throat. I wanted to cry, but I had halted tears before they formed by being angry instead. "I'm one-hundred percent positive I'm no good for you and your reputation." I had believed that from the start, but he had convinced me, for a short while, of the opposite.

"I'm positive."

I deflated, my anger disappearing in a puff of smoke. Hearing the words straight from his mouth, having this way out in the open and not a sad tale about my past, made everything a little better. "I'm sorry. I only want to do what's right for us." I turned my face up to him so he knew I was serious. I didn't want to hurt him or see him harmed because of me.

"Don't worry about it. This is a stressful situation, and you always have two different reactions for stress. You either get angry or you withdraw. I actually prefer the anger." He laughed as he pulled me into a hug. "Let's get dressed and go to a local café. I want to spend the holiday with you, Fuji-ko." He pressed his lips against my temple and squeezed me again. "I'll figure something else out."

CHAPTER
FOUR

So much for that vacation I was so excited about.

I paid for coffee and sandwiches and brought them to a little table near the front of the cafe where Yasahiro waited for me while he clicked around on his phone. As I approached him from across the room, I was struck by how in control he appeared to be, even when he wasn't talking to anyone or doing anything. He was wearing a black turtleneck, his hair a mess, and his glasses on, yet he still looked like he had stepped out of a magazine.

I set the cups on the table, and he smiled up at me, just a flash of grin before he was looking at his phone again. I sat opposite him and sipped at the warm brew, letting the coffee warm me from the inside out. I had only soaked in the bath at the onsen for maybe five minutes, and it wasn't enough to keep the winter chill away.

As I sipped and stared out the window, I remembered Mom and her worried frown. I guessed she'd had a right to be concerned. She was like a barometer for trouble. I should've listened to her.

"Mmm, the coffee is good, no?" Yasahiro asked, sipping with one hand and swiping with another.

"Sure. What are you looking at?"

"Other hotels in the area." He sighed and set the phone down. "I'm afraid I'm a bit of a snob when it comes to accommodations, and most of the five-star resorts are sold out."

I kept my smile small. "You don't say? You? A snob?" I quirked my lips at him.

"You hadn't noticed?" He laughed, and we both sipped our coffees to hide our humor.

"Tell me something..."

I set my cup down and folded my arms across my chest to keep warm. I shivered and Yasahiro reached into his bag on the floor and handed me a cashmere scarf. I held it up to him before putting it around my neck.

"See this? It's nothing but the best of things for you — an upscale, modern, professionally decorated apartment with all the amenities that's photographed for a Tokyo newspaper; a cashmere scarf from Paris; the finest Italian clothes; only the best ingredients for your restaurant." He sat still, not reacting to my long list of luxury items he owned. "Why would you want to date me when you won't even pick up a banana at the grocery store if it has a fleck of brown on it? It hasn't escaped my notice that I'm probably the most imperfect thing you could ever have."

Once I started living with Yasahiro part time, I saw how perfect his world was. I had never known anyone like him, someone without surface imperfections. Deep inside, I knew he had doubts about himself and his career, but those did not extend to his daily life.

"First of all," he said, warming his hands on his cup, "I do not *have* you. One does not own another person. My sense of perfection and... vanity — " He cleared his throat at this and my face grew hot "— only extends to objects, not people. There's something so gratifying about a flawless apple or having the exact amount of space in an apartment, or when I cut a hard-boiled egg in half and it's cooked to perfection. People are flawed. I'm flawed. You're flawed. There are no perfect people. Trust me. I believed I was going to marry the perfect woman, but it turned out she was rotten inside."

I froze at the mention of his ex-girlfriend, Amanda. I tried never to think of her, and he hadn't mentioned her in weeks, not since we slept together.

"What's on the surface doesn't count. I want the whole package, inside and out, to be worthy of my attention and love. The shiny apple doesn't make the cut if it tastes like sawdust. The symmetrical box gets rejected if the inside smells like something died in it."

"And me?" I picked up my cup again and sipped, the strong, sweet coffee, finally the right temperature.

"You only had to smile at me and I was hooked." He tilted his head to the side, and I was charmed by his glasses, casual sweater, and the way he gripped his mug. I was gone for him.

My chest ached with pride. "And if I change? What then?"

"I'm enjoying this philosophical conversation, Mei, but why can't you accept that I'm attracted to you? Really. I'm not lying."

He rubbed his leg up against mine. I was actually quite curious about his mindset and how he made decisions that affected his success, so my questions always delved into how he parsed and acted on the world around him. Plus, somewhere along the way, I doubted my own self-worth (after being laid off or fired five times in a row, how could I not?) so I also wondered why he would consider me a "good bet." I glanced away from him and out the window. In the end, his answers had little to do with why we were attracted to one another.

"No, I'm sure you're not lying." I smiled at him and squeezed his knee under the table. "I'll stop. I need to learn to accept things and not question why. There's not always a concrete answer to every question."

"Well, to answer your other question, people change all the time. I do. You do. Learning to accept and adapt to changes is a hard skill to master. But people don't change overnight, and it's easier when the change is gradual, unlike a natural disaster striking and turning your world upside down overnight."

Living in the land of earthquakes, this was always a fear of mine.

Yasahiro's phone rang, a chipper, tinkling tune, while it vibrated away on the table.

"Ah, good," he said, smiling at the screen. He swiped his phone on and answered. "Hiromi, thanks for calling me back... Yes, yes, we're in Hakone, but we're in a bit of a bind... Well, the hotel we were at is... unacceptable. Unfortunately, the woman who runs it has a major attitude." He winked at me. So this was our story? "I was hoping you could point me somewhere else?" He paused for a long moment, turning his mug around several times. "Oh wow, that *is* unfortunate... I see. Really? ... Hmmm, okay, let me talk it over with Mei, and I'll get back to you. Thanks."

He hung up, and I leaned forward to get the news.

"So here's where our situation can totally change," he said, spinning his phone on the table. "We can do one of two things. We can go home?"

I shrugged my shoulders. "I'd rather stay if we can."

"Or we can go to Hiromi's guesthouse and help out there. Her live-in staff member had to go home suddenly and care for her aging mother. That leaves her room free, but the guesthouse is booked solid, and they need help today getting ready for tonight and tomorrow."

Hmmm. This was supposed to be a vacation for the two of us to spend time together. Working through it for someone else didn't sound very relaxing.

But I looked across the table at his eager eyes and thought about how he wanted to spend time with me. It couldn't be that bad. I bet we'd have fun, actually.

"Sounds like a plan!" I gathered up our bags.

"Yes, let's head over there now. You'll love Hiromi and Andrew and their onsen. I promise it'll be fun." He kissed me on my temple, and with his arm over my shoulder, I believed him.

CHAPTER
FIVE

"What a beautiful place!" My breath caught in my chest as we walked in the door. Yoshitomo was a bright and happy guesthouse, a vibrant mix of traditional Japanese house and modern European architecture with a white Christmas tree sparkling in the corner of the entrance hall. The house smelled of cinnamon and clove, and quiet classical music drifted through the hallway.

"Yasahiro!" A young woman in her early thirties burst through a door, smiling and holding out her arms for a hug. Yasahiro dropped our bags and entered her embrace easily.

"Hiromi, it's so good to see you," he said, pulling away after a squeeze. "I'm sorry I haven't been here in a year. I should've come by during the summer."

She waved her hand and smiled. "It's fine. The year has been busy for everyone." She looked past him to me, so I bowed. "Is this Mei?"

"It is." He smiled as a wave of comfort washed over me. I had a feeling this was not the first time he'd mentioned me to her besides the phone call earlier. "Mei Yamagawa, this is Hiromi Pierce." We bowed to each other and she gave a very sly side-eye to Yasahiro. He cleared his throat. "I'm sure Andrew is here somewhere, right?"

His eyes widened in desperation, so she gestured behind her to a hallway. "He's in the kitchen, of course. Where else would he be?" She reached for our bags. "Welcome to Yoshitomo. Let me take you to your room. It's nice to meet you, Mei. I've been telling Yasahiro to bring you here since he told us about you in October, but he's been keeping you to himself."

"It's nice to meet you, too." October? We'd only just met in October! That was a good sign. Perhaps this meant something?

She led us down the hallway past community rooms and other bedrooms in disarray. It looked like the people staying here had dressed and left in a hurry.

"I'm sorry your room is not very big, and all of Sayako's belongings are in here. She said she was fine with you using her room, though, so don't worry about it."

Hiromi opened the door of a room tucked way in the back of the guesthouse next to the bathroom. It was only about three tatami mats in size, tiny compared to the five-star hotel. Sayako's photos and posters hung on the walls, her dressing table over-flowing with makeup and perfume.

"I've brought in a fresh futon for you. I'm sorry again." She bowed as we swept our eyes over the room. "I know you probably booked a suite at the last place."

Yasahiro grabbed her hand and squeezed it. "It's fine. Really. It's more than enough space for the two of us."

"Thank you so much," I said, setting my bag next to the futon closet door. "It's nice of you to accommodate us on such short notice."

"I'll let you get settled in, but please come meet us in the kitchen when you're ready." She backed out of the room and slid the door shut behind her.

Yasahiro let out a long sigh and sank to the floor. "This is not what I expected to happen today. I'm so sorry."

I kicked his foot. "Why are *you* sorry?" I dragged my bag across the room and set it against the far wall. "This was my first vacation in five years, and I ruined it. I was looking forward to that private bath."

I looked down at him, his head against the wall, a weary grin on his face. "Me too. I'll make it up to you. I promise."

We left our bags in the room and made our way through the guesthouse. Yasahiro showed me where the bathrooms were, the exits to the outside onsen hot spring baths (also called *rotenburo*), and he opened the door to the outside garden.

"It's a lovely place. I wish we could stay as guests instead of helpers."

"Maybe some other time," I said, slipping my arm around his waist. We spent two minutes breathing in the cold, winter air and staring out at the landscape, before heading to the kitchen.

We opened the door and were struck with the bustle of the kitchen in full swing. Special box lunches lined the stainless steel island awaiting morsels of treats for New Year's Day lunch tomorrow. The pungent tang of seaweed hung in the air as pots boiled away on the stove. Before long, treats like bitter oranges, black soybeans, mochi rice cakes wrapped in seaweed, and grilled fish cakes would be loaded in and ready to eat after a morning trip to the temple. Everyone looked forward to *osechi*, traditional New Year's Day lunch.

A Caucasian man was hunched over the stove, stirring away, while Hiromi chopped vegetables at the island. This must be Andrew, a friend of Yasahiro's from his days studying cuisine in Paris.

"Yasahiro! My man!" Andrew called out in English. He set down his spoon and crossed the room, engulfing Yasahiro in a bear hug that lifted him off the floor. He dwarfed us both, broad-shouldered and tawny hair tucked behind his ears under a chef's hat. "I'm so glad you came! Though I'm sorry to hear the circumstances, somehow I'm not surprised. You must be Mei. It's nice to meet you."

He offered a hand to shake and bowed at the same time. I did both, letting out a nervous giggle. I hoped I could remember my English.

"It's nice to meet you too," I stammered out, and he smacked himself upside the head.

"Sorry!" He switched to Japanese. "Yasahiro and I always spoke English in Paris. It wasn't until I met Hiromi that I learned the language."

Hiromi glanced up from chopping to smile. "He came here on vacation, and we fell in love."

The two looked at each other, and my heart warmed with their obvious affection.

"So, tell us how we can help," I reminded them, bowing again. "I'm an absolute disaster in the kitchen, but I can clean." I pointed to the mountain of pots and pans in the sink. "Let me get started there."

Hiromi paused for a second, no doubt her manners warring between having me relax as a guest and doing the work we promised to do by coming here and crashing their last unexpectedly open room.

"That would be a great help. Thank you."

"Fantastic." I got to business scrubbing and rinsing for a solid hour, humming to myself and listening to the conversation as Andrew and Yasahiro talked about old times and working in Paris.

After an hour of washing dishes and making sure everything was in order in the kitchen, I volunteered to clean up the guest rooms since it was unthinkable to go into the New Year with a house in disarray. Everyone cleaned in December to make sure their new year was full of good luck and cheer. I didn't want Hiromi and Andrew saddled with bad luck.

I had lived with bad luck my entire life and knew what that felt like. No one else should have to be stuck with that if I could help it.

Visiting each room, I emptied the trash and sorted it, moved the guests' bags to the walls, and vacuumed the tatami mats. Once the rooms were clean, I dusted the floors in the main hallways and wiped them down with a damp cloth.

By the time I was done, I was a sweating dirty mess, but the guest house was clean. I returned to the door to the garden, opened it to let fresh air in, and sat with my legs dangling over the side of the porch. I leaned against the door frame, wishing I was leaning against Yasahiro's shoulder instead. How was this any better than being at home? Though I was happy to help out these friends of Yasahiro's, I wished we had gone home to Chikata. This was my vacation, the first one I'd taken in five years. I glanced at the dirty rag next to me and sighed.

But maybe I was here because I was needed. Maybe this was where I was supposed to be. Maybe? I didn't know, and I wasn't sure of anything. Whatever the circumstances, we were here, and I needed to make the best of it.

I raised my shoulders. This was no time for self pity. Sure the last few months had been awful, but things could be worse, right?

For some reason, that didn't make me feel any better.

CHAPTER
SIX

I carried the bags of trash and the dirty rags into the chaotic kitchen. The box lunches for tomorrow were taking shape with morsels of gorgeous looking food lining several bento boxes. Yasahiro stood at the stove cooking up a thick omelette, his face peaceful and focused on his task. Even when he goes on vacation, he can't avoid spending time in the kitchen. I knew he didn't mind helping, but I'd hoped he could get time off for three days. I didn't feel three days was that much to ask for.

"I'm done cleaning the guesthouse. It's perfect, and you'll go into the new year ready for good luck," I said, placing the trash bags in the cubby off the kitchen and dumping the rags in the dirty wash bin. I glanced at the clock on the far side of the room, 15:15. "I'm a sweaty mess now, though."

Hiromi looked up from arranging pieces of food in the box lunch. "Ah, Mei. You've done so much work. I don't know how to repay you."

I waved my hand at her. "You don't have to. We're happy we have someplace to stay for New Year's Eve. It was my pleasure to help out." She didn't need to know I wished we'd gone home.

Hiromi and Andrew seemed like nice people, and it wasn't their fault my vacation was more of a work holiday. I should've been more proactive about choosing our hotel. Maybe if I had just admitted what I thought could happen, this might have been avoided.

But there was no use dwelling on things that had already happened.

"If it's okay, I'd like to get cleaned up and use the outdoor onsen before the guests arrive. But only if that's okay with you, though. If you have more work for me to do, I can postpone." I imagined the hot water soaking my aches and pains away. Hopefully, Yasahiro and I could enjoy them together later.

"Of course!" Hiromi smiled and waved towards the bathrooms. "You deserve it." She glanced at Yasahiro who was finishing the omelette. "We're almost done with the box lunches for tomorrow. Andrew and I can probably cover dinner between us. Yasahiro, why don't you join Mei?"

Yasahiro's eyebrows jumped, and his face relaxed. "That sounds like an excellent idea, but I have a few more things Andrew wanted me to do. It'll take maybe fifteen to twenty more minutes?"

"Then meet me out there," I said, smiling in his direction. Oh, this would be heavenly, and we could pick up our vacation where we left off.

Hiromi's phone jumped and vibrated on the stainless steel island. She dusted off her hands on a kitchen towel and bent over the phone to see who was calling. "Oh no," she said, rushing to answer it. "Mom, I'm so sorry... Yes. I know I forgot." She sighed, closing her eyes and pinching the bridge of her nose. "I meant to send Andrew an hour ago, but we've been swamped since we lost two helpers today... I know it's no excuse. I'm sorry. I'll drop everything and come to get you... You have more errands to run?"

She sighed again, and I waited, worried about how stressed she looked. "Yes, yes. I'll be there soon."

"Did we forget about your mother?" Andrew asked, cooking green beans in a wok at the stove.

"Yes we did. And I still have too much work to do between the box lunches and dinner tonight to go pick her up and shuttle her around." She looked over at me. "I'm sure you're not that big of a mess in the kitchen..."

Both Yasahiro and I laughed at the same time.

"I'm absolutely, completely, utterly incompetent in the kitchen. I can barely make rice. Isn't that right, Yasahiro?" I tried not to laugh too hard at myself. I should've been ashamed of how poor of a cook I was, but I had given up on that dream years ago. You can only set fire to the kitchen so many times before you give up.

"She's right. I plan to teach her knife skills soon, but I have to make sure my first aid kit at home is stocked beforehand." His smirk was one of the sexiest things I had ever seen.

"Ha ha. I'm dating such a joker." I winked at him.

Hiromi didn't smile, and her forehead crinkled with stress. "Okay. I'll put this aside and handle it later, if I can."

I had just met her a few hours ago, but I could tell by the set of her mouth, she was worried she wouldn't get her work done. I'd been in her shoes a million times and wished someone had helped me out. No one should be this stressed for the holiday.

If I could help, I would.

"Don't worry about it," I said, waving to the chopping board in front of her. "You stay here and take care of this. I'll go take care of your mom."

Both Hiromi and Andrew froze. Yasahiro, used to me doing this, returned to his omelette.

"Hmmm, Mei, that's really generous of you to offer, but you

don't know my mother. She's a bit... cantankerous and set in her ways. She would do nothing but give you a hard time. I should go."

She got as far as unbuttoning her apron before I could react and stop her. Cantankerous and set in her ways? That sounded like a challenge I was up for.

"No, really. I'm good with older folks, and it would be my pleasure to take care of your mom. You have enough work and stress here without having to deal with your mother too. Just let me get cleaned up, and I'll borrow Yasahiro's car to go meet up with her."

Andrew's jaw was locked open. "I don't think you want to do that. She's a really tough crowd."

Maybe I was getting myself into trouble, but if Hiromi left to deal with her mom, Yasahiro would spend more time in the kitchen. Then I wouldn't be spending time with him. There was no way I would sit around while everyone else worked.

And I loved a good challenge. I might as well spend the time with someone who needed me.

"I can handle a tough crowd. Not to worry."

I left them and returned to our room, determined to make someone happy this holiday, and I would start with Hiromi's mom. Picking out a new outfit, I cleaned up and changed in the bathroom, checked in with Hiromi, and left the guesthouse to find Hiromi's mother, Nahoko Nishimura.

———

I DROVE UP TO THE CONVENIENCE STORE IN TOWN AND parked the car. Inside the lit up window, blinking with Christmas lights, a little, old woman, her hair covered by a handkerchief and her arms weighed down with bags, stood peering out into the parking lot. Her face was set in a stern expression, and it reminded me of the day I met one of my own elderly clients for the first time. No one wanted to put trust in a complete stranger. I had to remember that.

I jumped out of the car and waved to her in the window. She didn't acknowledge me, except to narrow her eyes. *Remember to be polite, Mei.* I smiled as I came through the sliding doors.

"Hello! You must be Nahoko Nishimura, Hiromi's mother. I'm Mei Yamagawa, and I'm here to take you where you need to go." I bowed to her, showing the proper amount of respect, and held out my hands. "Can I take your bags? They look heavy."

"Get away from me," she growled, and I was reminded of a tiny, vicious dog at the end of its leash. "I'm not giving my bags to a stranger. I don't care who you are. I'm waiting here for my daughter."

Reaching into my pocket, I pulled out my phone and looked at it. No messages. If Hiromi was coming, she would've phoned me.

"I just came from Yoshitomo. Hiromi is swamped with work to do for the New Year celebration tonight. You're coming, right? I'm sure you'll enjoy all the wonderful food she and Andrew are preparing." She didn't answer me, her lips pressed into a thin line. "She sent me to pick you up and help you run errands. Didn't she call you?"

She curled her hands closer to her body with her bags. "I told her to come herself. When family needs help, you come. You don't send someone else to do your job for you."

Did she not have any idea how stressed out her daughter was?

"Well, that's not very fair. Everyone has jobs to do, and my job is to help other people who are too busy to do everything. And that's why I'm here."

She wouldn't budge. She kept a tight grip on her bags, and she leaned to the side to make eye contact with the store employee.

I held back a smile. She was really worried I was there to rob her or something, but I couldn't take it to heart. She didn't know me, and I didn't know her. There had to be a way I could get her to trust me.

I pulled Yasahiro's car keys from my pocket. "If you'd like, I can drive you directly to Yoshitomo. Just think of me as a taxi service, and I'll get you there."

"But I have more errands to run, and Hiromi promised me she'd drive me around today." She looked desperate for her daughter. I had to reel her back in.

"I'm sure that was before Sayako had to go take care of her ailing mother, and her other employee called in sick. She's doing the work of three people. Even I cleaned the guesthouse today, and I'm supposed to be on vacation." I laughed, looking around the convenience store and thinking about grabbing a snack. All that hard work had made me hungry. "I'm going to grab a sandwich and a drink. Would you like something before we take off?"

She sighed, setting her bags on the floor next to her. "I'll have cold green tea. The kind with the green label, not the white one. And a tuna rice ball."

I paused, my hand reaching into my purse for my wallet. "Anything else?"

"No."

Not even a thank you. She *was* a tough crowd.

I walked around the store, browsing the fast and easy foods I had given up since meeting Yasahiro, the slow food haute cuisine boyfriend that he was. It never stopped me from craving my favorite salt and seaweed potato chips or chocolate covered almonds, though. I had no time to pick up a chicken curry ramen bowl, but an egg salad sandwich was a good idea. A tuna rice ball and green tea for Nahoko went into my basket as well.

The cashier rung me up and bowed as I returned to Nahoko.

"Come! We can eat in the car with the heat blasting, and you can tell me where we're off to first." I smiled and walked out the door, like any mother of small children would, thinking they'd follow.

"Wait! Mei, is it?" she called out from behind me.

I paused at the sliding doors.

"Can you carry these bags? They're too heavy for me."

I blew out a relieved breath and turned around to face her.

"Of course. Let's get these in the car so we can be on our way."

CHAPTER
SEVEN

Our first stop was a saké brewery and distributor. The monstrous building took up half the block, dark wood outer walls looming over the streets and a giant cedar ball hanging in the doorway. The inside was lit with Christmas lights and music played outside the front door.

"What a beautiful building," I said, leaning forward over the steering wheel to peer out the front windshield. I parked Yasahiro's car in an empty spot in the lot. Oh, I adored shopping! Though I didn't shop often with my lack of funds, I still loved when I brought home something fresh and new. There was bound to be a gift here for Mom. She loved saké.

Nahoko barely looked at me, her arms folded over her purse in her lap. "I'll get out here. You should stay in the car." She unlocked the doors and let herself out.

"Wait!" I lunged sideways hoping to catch her attention. She slammed the door and walked away.

"You should stay in the car," I mumbled, mocking her stern attitude. Sheesh. When Andrew said she was a tough crowd, I didn't think she would be this bad. Usually people warmed up to me pretty quickly. My mom had taught me good manners, and I always put on a smile, even when things were horrible.

It wasn't me, it was her.

Turning off Yasahiro's car, I sat in the wintry silence. I drummed my fingers on the steering wheel while the warm air vanished from the car. Had Yasahiro texted me yet? Nope. My messages app was absent any notifications. He was probably deep into frying up shrimp or something else, talking with his friends, and having fun while I was sitting in the car like a chauffeur.

Whatever, lady. I wasn't going to sit in the car waiting for her. My mom and I loved saké. I would head inside to see if I could find anything worth buying for myself.

When the doors to the brewery slid open, I brightened at the sheer enormity of the place. Shelves of saké, shochu, and other liquors lined the floor space, and I grinned, wondering what treasures I would find here.

I snaked up and down the rows, reading labels and checking prices, while the warm air soaked into my coat and body.

"I told you to stay in the car," Nahoko said, approaching me with two bottles of saké in her arms. A weary young man followed behind her, his arms laden with more bottles.

"Well, my mom and I love saké, and I thought I'd bring a bottle home to her as a New Year's gift." It was bad enough I wasn't there with her for the holiday. I should return home with booze to smooth things over.

I looked past Nahoko and smiled at the young man, radiating sympathy towards him. With his dark-rimmed eyes and crazed hair, he was someone who'd had his fill of the holiday season.

"Oh no," Nahoko chided me, "don't you dare steal my salesman. I have four more bottles to buy."

I raised my hands. "Don't worry. I wasn't about to steal him." I moved past her to the young man. "I can take these to the register for you. That way, you can help her with the last few bottles she needs."

He sighed in relief, his shoulders dropping. "Thank you so much."

I took the bottles from him and smiled at Nahoko as I shuffled past her. She narrowed her eyes at me, watching me all the way to the cash register, making sure I didn't do anything with her bottles. I set them to the side and then went to browse for myself.

"Don't leave my bottles unattended!" Nahoko yelled across the store.

I halted in my tracks and returned to the register to wait. Really, was it too much to ask for a "please?"

I waited close to the counter, looking up and down the aisles from my spot. I wanted to pick up two bottles of a dry saké, something that would go nice with winter hot pots full of vegetables, mushrooms, and fish.

Now that I was dating Yasahiro, I thought more about food and how to pair it with what to drink. This was one of his favorite things to do, pair a beer or saké with a specific dish. I imagined us back in his apartment at home, standing in the kitchen, laughing and drinking while soup bubbled away on the stove. I hoped January would bring us closer together since the last month had not gone well. We hadn't spent enough time together in December, but January would be free of obligations and travel. And since I was practically living at his place, we could spend the cold winter nights in bed.

I drifted off in thought, remembering his warm skin against mine, the lightness of his touch, and his kiss drifting down my cleavage...

"What are you over here smiling about?" Nahoko jumped into my daydream, knocking me out of my dirty thoughts and straight back into the brewery.

"Nothing," I said, clearing my throat. "Are you finished?"

"Don't be rude. I'll be done when I'm done." She frowned at me, and I took a step away from her hostility. "Yes. I'm done."

Well, all she had to do was say she was finished, not give me a lecture. Did she think I was a child?

I drew in a deep breath. *Don't be snippy, Mei.* I had to remember that she wasn't my mother, and I was only helping out. I could put up with her attitude for a few more hours.

"Okay. While he's ringing you up, I'll grab my bottles of saké."

I turned to walk away, but she interrupted me.

"You're going to leave me here with all of these bottles?" Her voice rose in astonishment.

She was testing me, I knew it. I wondered if she did this with everyone. Was she intentionally rude to see how far she could push me? I suspected most people gave her what she wanted.

Not me.

"Seeing as you asked me to wait in the car in the first place, I'm sure you can handle paying for the saké on your own. I'll pick out my two bottles, pay, and then I'll help you carry your saké to the car."

I walked away before she could argue with me anymore. It was best to cut her off before she got into it any further.

Browsing up and down the aisles, I found two dry saké varieties from Iwate prefecture. Both seemed like good choices, and I couldn't wait to show them to Yasahiro. It was silly but their well-designed labels and pretty bottles appealed to me. I was sure he would like them too.

On my way back to the front of the store, I grabbed one more bottle for the evening. This one would be for just the two of us.

"I thought you were only going to buy two bottles," she said, as I paid the young man at the counter.

"I changed my mind. They all look delicious, and I wanted something extra for tonight."

She harrumphed, grabbing two bags of saké and leaving the rest for me. "Don't take too long." She headed for the door without saying anything else.

I fished through my pocket for Yasahiro's keys, clicked the remote start button, and unlocked the car doors. At least she could let herself in and sit in the warmth until I got there.

"She's my toughest customer," the young man whispered at me. "She knows what she wants, when she wants it, and if we don't have it, she gets upset. I once had to drive fifty kilometers to retrieve a special bottle for her. I missed my girlfriend's holiday party." He sighed wearily as he hefted the boxes under his arms.

"Somehow, I'm not surprised."

CHAPTER
EIGHT

Our second stop of the day was at a grocery distributor off the main strip. I fell in love with the cheery storefront and happy customers leaving as we pulled into the parking lot. This was the holiday cheer that had been missing from my life recently.

"What are you picking up here?" I asked, parking the car.

Nahoko opened the car door. "Citrus gift boxes," she said with a sigh. "Are you going to stay here or are you going to come in with me this time?"

I chewed on my lip, thinking over my options. I could stay in the car, return email, surf the web, or write to Yasahiro, or go inside and look for more New Year's gifts for my family and friends. If this place was good enough for Nahoko, who appeared to have rigorous standards, I was sure I would find something that'd be nice for my mom or Yasahiro.

I also wanted to help Nahoko, but I didn't want to annoy her. And it seemed like I did nothing but annoy her.

I was grasping for any excuse to go into the store with her, obviously.

"I'll come with you." I turned off the car and came around to the passenger side to help her out. She refused to take my hand, so I helped her up by the crook of her arm.

"I can get out of the car on my own, you know. I'm not some invalid." Just the sound of her voice was grating on me.

I flashed back to Hiromi and Andrew's faces when I volunteered myself into this fresh hell. I should've learned to read people better.

"I didn't say you were an invalid. I'm just trying to be nice, which you don't seem to appreciate." My heart raced at my bold words, but I knew it was a mistake immediately.

She threw my hand off her arm. "You don't get to tell me what I can or can't appreciate. You're a very presuming young lady. It's no wonder you're not married." She twirled around as best as an old lady could and huffed off into the store.

"Great job, Mei," I mumbled to myself. I was doing a horrible job of making friends with her. I needed to find some common ground or this would end badly.

I threw back my shoulders and lifted my head, determined to get in there and make the most of this awful situation. *Remember, Mei. You got yourself into this in the first place.*

The inside of the store was warmer than outside but still chilly enough to keep the fruits and vegetables fresh for customers. I steeled myself as I approached Nahoko, chatting amiably with the store's owner as he stacked boxes for her at the cash register. He bowed and held up one finger to show he'd help me after he finished with her.

"It's all right. I'm here to help Mrs. Nishimura."

"My daughter was unable to be here with me today, so she sent this ungrateful woman in her place. She has done nothing but bug me for the past hour." Nahoko's eyes remained firm as she stared me down, challenging me to speak out against her.

I wanted to tell her to take the bus home, but I promised I would do what I could. Why was she so mean? I didn't understand how anyone could go through life being this sour. But I wasn't one to break my promise, even when I was being treated this poorly. One more outburst from her, though, and I was returning to the car to be on my own in blessed silence.

"I'm sure this young lady is doing everything she can to help you out," the man said, and I cheered silently for him. If Nahoko was a regular customer here, he understood my predicament, most likely.

"Are these the citrus gift boxes you're going to buy?" I stood on my tiptoes to peer into the top box. Beautifully symmetrical and round, each variety of citrus fruit was nestled into white and gold straw, the boxes wrapped in a red ribbon. "Ah! These are beautiful! I'm sure they'll make great gifts for your family and friends."

The shop owner swelled with pride. "Thank you so much. We're very pleased with this year's varieties. Would you like to buy one for yourself?"

Nahoko stepped between us. "You ring me up first, and then you can help her." I rolled my eyes at Nahoko behind her back, and the shopkeeper smiled at me.

"Of course, I'll help you first." He maneuvered around to the other side of the cash register. "In the meantime, please have a look at the boxes and see if anything strikes you as suitable."

I glanced at the price tags on Nahoko's boxes as I pushed them towards her. Yikes. They were three times more expensive than I expected them to be.

"Oh, on second thought, I'll have to skip them this year, though they're very beautiful. I'm afraid I was stupid and spent my budget for gifts too swiftly." My mom always taught me that when I was in a pinch and a burden on someone else, I should blame the problems on myself. I didn't have to feel ashamed, but I should make an appearance of taking the blame so as not to embarrass the other person. It was something I did naturally that drove Yasahiro crazy, but it was a hard habit to break.

"Stupid, huh? I don't find that surprising at all."

Oof, it felt like a dagger to the heart. Just because I said I was stupid didn't mean other people could call me that. But maybe I *was* stupid? How did someone like me with an education and a good, solid upbringing lose her job over and over? My bad luck was due to my foolishness, right?

My face fell into a deep frown, all the holiday cheer leached from me in one swift statement.

"You don't even know me," I whispered, unable to raise my voice any higher. Sickness roiled in my gut, a storm churning and threatening to take away any semblance of happiness I had left. "I'll be in the car."

The store was a blur as I made for the door, trying to walk as fast as possible without losing my cool in front of anyone else. I splashed through slush and snow as I approached the car, stopping to look at my reflection in the car window.

Wait. I was a good person. Sure, I wasn't the smartest person around, nor was I the prettiest or the fastest or most talented or whatever. I was mediocre in so many ways. But I prided myself on being resourceful when I needed to be, being kind when all else failed, or being helpful when it mattered most.

If I couldn't win this woman over, how was I going to make this whole senior-center tea shop work? I wouldn't just be catering to people I already knew. I would meet new people who didn't trust me but needed to, just like Nahoko.

I got in the car and started it up, turning the heat on full blast, and reclining my seat to rest. Light from the parking lot overhead lamps shined down on me, highlighting the dusting of new snow swirling through the air.

In my pocket, my phone buzzed.

"How are you? I'm a little worried I haven't heard from you in over an hour," Yasahiro wrote.

"I'm okay. Hiromi's mom is worse than I expected though. She's not very nice."

He texted a frowning face and then, *"Come back to me. I miss you. I'm done in the kitchen and I thought we'd spend an hour together before dinner."*

I was so tempted to just leave. Nahoko had burned through all my good will, and I wanted to spend time with someone who loved me and cared for me, someone who would make me happy, not annoyed and angry.

I groaned as I thought about poor Hiromi, weighed down with cooking and entertaining. The guests at the guesthouse had probably returned from their outings and were enjoying the hot baths. Even if Hiromi wasn't busy in the kitchen, she'd be busy doing the other things her usual but absent staff members would handle.

Staring down at Yasahiro's text, I knew what I had to do.

"She has one more place she needs to go and then I can come back. I'll make it quick. Save a spot for me in the hot bath."

He texted, *"I'm not getting in without you. I'll wait for you at the front door."* Heart emoji.

I smiled at the text and turned off the phone before I got teary eyed. He was too good to me.

Tap tap tap at the window. And there went my good cheer.

"Are you going to get out and help me with this?" Nahoko's voice rang through the car.

That was it! I'd had it with her poor attitude. I popped the trunk and jumped out of the warm car.

"You don't get any more help from me unless you say please or thank you," I said, and her face closed up. "I came out here today to help you out of the goodness of my heart. I did not come here to be abused by you."

She adjusted the handkerchief on her head and opened her mouth, but I held up my hand. I was tired of her excuses for being rude.

I circled around the car, took her bags, and added them to the bags in the back seat, saying nothing. The man who assisted us inside came out with two more bags and I had him put them in the trunk. He said goodbye to Nahoko, and I got in the car and waited for her.

"Now," I said, buckling my seatbelt. "You have one more place to go? Let's get there and be done with this. My boyfriend is waiting for me at Yoshitomo. This is my first vacation in five years, and you are not going to ruin it."

"Fine. I need to go to the stationery store, and then we can be done."

Done couldn't come soon enough.

I started the car with a flick of my wrist and got us under way.

CHAPTER
NINE

The stationery store was on the opposite side of town from Yoshitomo. Of course. I had never felt so far away from my goals or my peace. It was as if I had been driving in circles all day, only for my destination to be always out of reach. Like one of those nightmares you can't wake up from where you walk the halls of your high school for hours and never find your homeroom.

Only I was awake, and this torture was of my own doing. First, I got us kicked out of our hotel. Then I volunteered to clean instead of relax, and now I'm chauffeuring the most bitter woman I've ever met.

I found a parking spot on the street outside of the store and parallel parked in one try. Why wasn't anyone ever around to witness it when I did that?

"I'll wait for you here. Try not to take too long," I said, turning off the car and unlocking the doors. I grabbed my phone and pretended to ignore her, hoping she'd take the hint I wouldn't be nice to her anymore.

She left the car without acknowledging me, slamming the

door behind her. Sigh. Hopefully, I'd be back to Yoshitomo within twenty minutes.

It wasn't too long before I was bored with my phone. All my emails had been returned, and I'd checked my social media networks.

So instead of mindlessly clicking around, I stared out at the darkened street and daydreamed. I tried to think of all the different things I wanted to do with the retail space below Yasahiro's apartment, how I would turn it into my senior center tea shop. The most expensive part of the renovation would be converting the bathroom and making it handicapped accessible, which I felt was necessary when dealing with an older population. Everything else I could do myself or get help from my mom, Kumi and Goro, and other volunteers.

I was imagining what colors to paint the walls when my unfocused eyes caught peculiar movement on the sidewalk. An older woman, possibly in her late eighties, hobbled along at a slow pace. She paused, turned around, and stopped, looking at the shop fronts in front of her. She turned and repeated, meandering, pausing, turning around. She looked like a six-year-old child searching for her mother in the grocery store, lost and alone.

I waited and watched her, but her movements remained consistent. She'd walk for a minute, pause, turn around, and squint at whatever sign was in front of her. I retrieved my phone from the car cupholder and brought up the local map. This being a touristy part of the city, I figured there had to be a police box nearby. Yeah, about six blocks away. I glanced up from my phone in time to see the woman make her way to the nearest intersection.

Oh no. She wasn't aware enough to navigate traffic.

I scrambled to get out of the car, making sure I didn't open my door into traffic. Hurrying along, I leapt over slushy puddles along two cars before jumping to the sidewalk curb.

"Excuse me. Are you okay?" I stopped her with a hand on her shoulder, and her face collapsed into frustration.

"I don't know where I am," she said, clutching her bag to her chest. She looked left and right before shaking her head. "I've been walking for a while, and I was supposed to meet my son, but I got turned around."

I glanced over at the stationery store, and Nahoko was paying for whatever she'd bought. She'd be done in a minute.

"Do you know where you were going to meet your son?" She was definitely lost, and I didn't want her stuck out in the winter weather when her family was worried about her. The sidewalk was dark, and with the temperatures low and clouds threatening to rain, walking outside would become dangerous soon.

"No," she said, sighing. "I thought I wrote it down, but I can't find it in my bag."

"What's going on out here?" Nahoko asked, approaching us. "Why are you disturbing this woman?"

I took a deep breath. I couldn't let her get to me now.

"I'm not disturbing her. She's lost and trying to meet her son, but she doesn't remember where she said she'd meet him." I rested a hand on the woman's shoulder. "There's a police box not far from here. Why don't I take you there? They can hopefully help you find your son."

"I don't know." She shivered, looking between Nahoko and me.

Nahoko sighed, waving the woman forward. "Come with us. Mei won't hurt you."

I raised my eyebrows at her and she huffed. I supposed that was the closest I would get to an apology.

Nahoko escorted the woman to the backseat of the car, and I

pushed Nahoko's bags to one side, moving a few to the trunk to make room. When I got behind the wheel, I gripped it tight and closed my eyes for a second. What else was going to happen today? How did a quick vacation morph into babysitting and rescuing old ladies from the street?

"Okay, let's get you over to the police." I started the car and used my phone to guide me the six blocks to the local police box. Like most people, I grew up trusting the police implicitly. If I had a problem or a question, I would also go to the police box to ask for their help, and they always gave it. If this woman lived around here or was visiting, the police could help, I was sure of it.

For the umpteenth time that day, I parked in another parking lot, and Nahoko and I helped the woman inside the police box building.

"Excuse me," I asked the police officer at the front desk. She smiled up at me. "I, uh, found this woman wandering the street not far from here. I think she's lost. Well, she thinks she's lost." I turned around, and she was drifting away from Nahoko towards the sliding glass door. "Oh no. Hold on."

I ran for her before she went outside, and the police officer followed me.

"Excuse me!" I called out to her, running in front of her before the door could open.

"I'm looking for my son. Do you know where he is?" she asked, her eyes blank, as if she'd never seen me before.

"No. I don't. And that's why we're here. Remember?"

She shook her head, and Nahoko sighed in the background.

"I found you wandering the streets and brought you here to the police."

"Who are you?" she asked, and the police woman nodded at her.

"This woman brought you here so you can find your family."

The officer's voice was strong but sympathetic. She turned to me, lowering her voice. "We see this all the time, especially in the evenings."

"Can we go now?" Nahoko asked, glancing at the clock on the wall. "You said we would just bring her here. She's here and now we can leave."

I bit my lip, wondering how involved I should get in this.

"Mom!" A frantic older man, his wife and older kids burst through the door and rushed to us, nearly knocking over the old woman. She took a moment to realize this was someone she knew and then she cried into his shoulder as they hugged. "We've been looking for you everywhere!"

"Oh good," I said, bowing to her family. "See? Your son wasn't too far away."

"Thank you," she replied, bowing back. "I wasn't sure what to do."

"What happened?" the man asked me, clutching his mother around her shoulders.

"I was sitting in my car waiting for my friend while she was in the stationery store, and I noticed your mom looked lost. That's all. I spoke to her, figured out what was going on, and brought her here."

"I'm so sorry for all the trouble." The man's wife joined us, her eyes red with tears. "She must've gotten turned around when it was time to leave the hotel for tea. We've been looking for her for the past hour."

"It was no trouble at all." I bowed to them, happy I took the time to trust my instincts and help this woman. "I'm glad you showed up. I was worried about leaving her here." I bowed again to the old woman. "Have a happy new year and stick close to your family."

"I will," she said, and we smiled at each other. At least one thing had gone right today.

I gestured to Nahoko that we should leave, and she followed me out the door.

"Okay, back to Yoshitomo," I said, opening Nahoko's door for her.

"Do you always do things like that? Pick old ladies off the street and deliver them back to their families?" Her eyes were deep pools looking straight into my soul. I hoped she saw I was a good person.

"At least once a week." I was joking and flicked a smile at her.

She didn't smile back, but by the tune of her sigh, I got the feeling she was slightly amused.

Ever so slightly.

It was something.

CHAPTER
TEN

Rain began to fall on the drive back to Yoshitomo, coating the road in a slippery slush and chilling me to the bone. I navigated the streets in silence, checking the map on my phone to make sure I was going in the right direction. Nahoko could've guided me but she wasn't speaking to me, and I couldn't figure out why. I thought maybe our trip back would be a little more cordial after returning the old woman to her family, but perhaps my hopes were too high. I knew nothing about Nahoko except for how she treated me all afternoon. She could have had plenty of reasons for being the bitter person she was. I didn't know. I only wanted to help out Hiromi.

I pulled into the driveway at Yoshitomo and parked the car straight up front.

"It's raining. I hope you have an umbrella," Nahoko said, her face turned away from me. I leaned over the divider between us to look in the front foot well and then in the back. No umbrella. Of course. It was probably in the trunk or we had left it at home this morning.

"It appears I don't. Sorry."

"Well, you had better run inside and get one."

I was about to snap at her for being rude when I heard a tap at the window. Yasahiro's smiling face was beaming down on me from outside, his head covered by an umbrella.

"Hi," I said, a sigh escaping. I was never so happy to see anyone in my entire life. I cracked the door, and he swung to the side to hold the umbrella over me as I popped out of the car.

"Hi, yourself. I've been waiting for you. I thought you'd be back twenty minutes ago," he said, reaching out for me. I jumped at him, throwing my arms around his neck and squeezing. A small sob leaked from my lips, the events of the afternoon finally catching up to me. "Oh, Mei. I'm sorry. Did you have a rough day?"

"The worst." I pushed the door closed with my hip. "I'm so glad to be back."

Yasahiro's face contorted from miserable to happy in one swift movement. Regret, I detected regret. "Mei Yamagawa, you're the best thing that's ever happened to me. I'm never letting a vacation like this happen again."

He leaned forward, and with his arm wrapped around my waist and the other keeping us dry with the umbrella, he pressed his lips to mine and stole my heart. This was what we should have been doing, sharing intimate moments, talking and eating and drinking and laughing, being together. I was supposed to spend this holiday with someone I loved. That was the most important thing on earth.

I let the kiss linger, enjoying the moment, and letting him take away my bad day with his attention. I drew in a deep breath through my nose before pulling away. His sigh and smile brought a blush straight up from my toes, and I pressed my forehead to his to ground myself.

"This is outrageous." My stomach flipped as Nahoko's words

sliced between Yasahiro and me. "How dare you leave me out in the rain while you do unseemly things with your boyfriend. I'm shocked and offended."

"Mom, you should've called first so I could meet you at the car." Hiromi rushed forward out of the shadow of Yoshitomo's front porch, rain boots on her feet but missing an umbrella. Her mother pushed past her, getting to shelter quickly.

"This is despicable treatment I get from a daughter who shirks her duties," Nahoko said, shedding her handkerchief once she was out of the rain. "You send a stranger to deal with me on one of the most auspicious family days of the year. We were supposed to spend today and tomorrow together as a family."

Hiromi's shoulders fell, and her eyes welled with tears. "I'm trying to keep the family business alive short on staff. Dad would not have wanted me to ignore my guests."

Andrew appeared in the doorway, his chef's whites smeared with food and a towel over his shoulder. "We've been busy all day taking care of the paying customers."

"It doesn't matter now what your father would've wanted." Nahoko rounded on Hiromi who shrank away from her. "And I can tell you this much, he would have been ashamed of you for treating me this way." She turned from her dumbstruck daughter to point at me. "You, bring in the bags from the car."

Andrew gasped, and Yasahiro's face blanked.

"No," he said, squeezing me to him. "I'll bring in your bags."

"And then we'll be leaving," I butted in, stepping forward. "You're right. This is an auspicious day, and it's important to spend it with family. So, we'll pack our things and go."

Nahoko nodded her head once. "Good."

It was Hiromi's turn to gasp. "Mom! That is not how we treat honored guests around here. What's gotten into you?"

I turned my head, ashamed to witness this private dispute,

even though it was mostly my fault. If only I had been better in the kitchen, Hiromi could've tended to her mother and I could've helped with the food. This is not the first time my lack of cooking skills has been detrimental to my life, but that shouldn't be a reason for Hiromi and Andrew to suffer.

"I'm in my last years, and you and your husband do nothing but ignore me. Where are my grandkids, huh? Why do you leave me in that house on the other side of town? We're supposed to be living together as a family. Shifting me off on a stranger is not how we do things."

I cringed and made eye contact with Yasahiro. He looked as uncomfortable as I felt. Perhaps everything wasn't my fault. I was just in the wrong place at the wrong time.

I could see the hurt in Hiromi's eyes and the hard set of Andrew's jaw. This was more personal than I expected Nahoko's homecoming to be.

She seemed pleased she had gotten her point across and pushed past Andrew into the guesthouse. He stood and stared at Hiromi and she looked at the ground, rain coating her hair and dripping down her face.

"I'm sorry," I said, bowing. "I'm not sure if I made things better or worse for you, and for that, I apologize." Hiromi stared at me, her eyes vacant. "If you like, we'd be happy to have you and Andrew for a visit to Chikata in the spring. There's a guest-house in town we can secure for you, and the countryside is really beautiful that time of year. I hope you'll consider it."

"Why would you ever want to see us again?" Hiromi asked, her voice raspy, astonished. "I'm horrified by what just happened, and by what you went through today."

I shook my head, beckoning her to join us under the umbrella. "I'll be fine. I don't have to live with her, but you do. Whatever she wants, you should look into it." I pressed my hand to my heart. "We only have so much time on this earth. Try to fill it with joy." I wasn't sure if those were the right words, but I figured they'd do.

"I'll bring in the packages. Mei, you'll go pack our things?"

He handed me the umbrella, and I put an arm around Hiromi. "Come on. Let's get back inside where it's dry."

CHAPTER
ELEVEN

The headlights of the highway smeared into one long, blurry mess as we made our way back home. I spent the time staring out the window and thinking of what had happened that day. It started out so hopeful and full of promise, falling to pieces as the day went on. We should have just gone home after being turned away at the first hotel. It was a bad sign we ignored because we needed a little vacation.

Yasahiro reached across the car and squeezed my hand. "You're more quiet than usual. I was thinking we'd stop for dinner. There's a roadside plaza ahead that has a great ramen restaurant."

"Sure. We should eat. I'm sorry you didn't get to eat any of the delicious food you made. They didn't even offer us an *osechi* lunchbox when we left. I'm afraid I've damaged your relationship with them permanently." My voice squeaked, catching in my throat. They had felt ashamed and so had we. It would be a miracle if we ever saw each other again.

He pulled his hand back, gripping the steering wheel before changing lanes. "I thought I had brought us to a safe place, some place where you and I would be welcome. Sure, I knew they would put us to work, but I figured it was an hour or two, and then we'd be on our own. I'm sorry I got us into this mess. The whole thing."

He exited the highway, pulling into the roadside plaza and finding a spot not too far from the restaurant. The rain was a gossamer veil draped over the world, no longer falling in sheets but instead blanketing everything in mist.

We ran into the ramen restaurant, bought our selections from the machine, and turned in our tickets, sitting down in an open booth. A woman stopped by to deliver two cups of green tea and hot towels for our hands. It was late for dinner, already past 20:00, but the restaurant had plenty of New Year's Eve travelers, eating, talking, and laughing. In only a few hours, January would be here, and I was more than ready to put this current year behind me.

"I can't believe I haven't asked this yet, but do you have any New Year's resolutions set?" I asked Yasahiro as I smoothed my curly hair, kinked by the moisture laden air. I was desperate for a good bath and shower, but it would have to wait until we got home.

He laughed, grabbing a napkin from the dispenser on the table and using it to wipe his glasses. "I'm not very good with resolutions. I wish I was. Everyone around me loves to make business plans and abide by them, but I'm more of a seat-of-the-pants kind of guy. I see opportunities, and I take them. There's no planning that." He sighed, rolling his head to stretch his neck. "But then, maybe things like today wouldn't happen, and we'd be sipping champagne from our private bath in a five-star hotel."

"You did plan the trip ahead of time, so try not to beat your-self up about it."

He looked straight through me, and I halted twirling my hair in my fingers.

"This was supposed to be a vacation for you, a way for you to feel warm, full of good food, and loved. I completely failed, and I have no idea why you're not angry."

Our bowls of ramen arrived, and I was grateful for the break. This happened too often between us when we each blamed ourselves for the bad luck in our relationship. I lived a life of bad luck, and before he met me, he was always prosperous. I thought the blame was clear, but he consistently had good reasons why it was his fault. This was something we argued about on a regular basis.

I leaned over the bowl and took a deep inhale. Ah, this was what I needed. We broke apart our chopsticks, said the ritual prayer, and dug in. The long chewy noodles and salty broth were heaven, warming me up from the inside out.

"I'm not angry with you," I said between slurps. I covered my mouth behind my hand to hide my chomping teeth. "You're the person who has treated me the nicest today. Well, you're the person who's treated me the nicest the past couple of months."

Yasahiro had nothing to say to that. His lips twisted, but he kept on eating.

"Aren't you going to ask me about my New Year's resolutions?" I said with a smile, nudging him under the table with my foot.

He laughed again, and it was nice to hear. Laughter had been very absent from my day. "So, Mei, do you have any New Year's resolutions?"

"I'm so glad you asked me this important question. You're going to laugh... But I want to learn to cook a few things this year."

He set his chopsticks down and folded his hands. "I'm not

going to laugh. This is somewhat shocking. What's gotten into you?"

My face heated, so I covered it up by eating more noodles. "Nothing's gotten into me. I just think I should learn to deal with cooking food. What if you travel again and I'm on my own? What if something like today happens again, and I can't help in the kitchen?"

"But you hate the kitchen," he said, a note of bewilderment in his voice.

"I don't hate the kitchen. I'm..." I remembered the time I was a teen, set fire to a wooden spoon, and then passed out.

"Terrified of the stove. And for good reason too. I've seen you in the kitchen. Your face whitens, you sweat, and your hands shake. You can boil water and make pasta but that's about it. Why would you want to do that to yourself?"

He's right, of course. Working in the kitchen is like torture, but...

"If I had skills to help out, maybe I wouldn't be so useless. You should've seen me today. I did everything in my power to help that woman. If I can't win her over, then how do I open a tea shop for the elderly and do well? I should concentrate on practical skills."

And there was the heart of the matter. Nahoko had crushed my confidence. She had shown me that no matter how hard I tried, I wouldn't get anywhere just by being polite and kind. I needed real skills. If I had helped out in the kitchen instead of going to help her, everyone would have been happier.

Yasahiro groaned and rubbed his face. "Mei, you have exceptional skills with the elderly. They practically flock to you. You're a good organizer and helper, and you help them live their lives. You're a people person through and through. Hiromi's mother? She missed out on a splendid day with you because she couldn't see past her own issues. That has nothing to do with you and everything to do with her. You'll open the best damned tea shop in town, the best in the prefecture. A place where people will feel welcome. A safe place. Don't falter now because of one bad experience. If I had given up when I got dressed down by a three-Michelin starred chef in front of the entire kitchen, I would never have opened Sawayaka. These things are meant to strengthen you, not pull you down."

I blinked, bulldozed over by his statements. I had never looked at my life that way, but I guessed he was right. The burns I experienced as a kid made me stronger. Getting fired several times had made me stronger. Going without food and heat had made me stronger. This would strengthen me too.

"You really think being a people person is a skill?"

"It's a gift. Few have that." He lifted his bowl and drank the soup, smacking his lips and sighing afterward. It *was* good soup.

"A gift," I whispered. Something I used for helping the elderly and for solving murders too, it seemed.

"But I have an idea," he said, raising one side of his lips. "If you want to learn some skills in the kitchen, I'll teach you prep work."

"Oh yes! Mom said I should learn knife skills."

He stood up from the table and buttoned up his coat. I followed, my soup already gone from the bowl.

"Your mom is right, naturally. Let's go home and tomorrow morning, we'll surprise everyone with something delicious to eat."

He slung his arm over my shoulder and kissed my temple as we made our way back out to the car.

CHAPTER
TWELVE

Back in Chikata, the local businesses were abuzz with parties and people spilling out of local izakayas, including our favorite, Izakaya Jūshi. Despite Etsuko's murder not too long ago, the whole neighborhood showed up to support her family for the holiday. The place was packed and white lights twinkled around the windows.

"Look," I said, pointing out the window. "They have a countdown. Only two more hours till the new year."

Yasahiro pulled into his parking spot and turned off the car. "Okay, here's what we're going to do," he said, clapping his hands together and exiting the car. I followed him out and bundled up against the cold winter wind. "We're going to get upstairs and then I will enact the new New Year's Eve plan."

This sounded intriguing, and I smiled, wondering what he had been thinking about all the way home. We had driven in silence, listening to music, and consulting the map when traffic got too heavy. Thank goodness the roads were clear, and we drove home quicker than we had to Hakone in the morning.

I couldn't believe everything that had happened in one day.

We'd started the trip so positively, ready for rest and relaxation, and we were beaten down as the day went on. I was glad to be home, even if it meant there would be no vacation for me.

I didn't need a vacation, it turned out. I needed peace.

I followed Yasahiro as he carried our bags up the stairs and opened his apartment.

The inside was chilly and dark as we entered, but with the flick of a few switches, the Christmas tree came to life, the lights illuminated, and the heat switched on. It would be homey and warm in no time.

"We could go to Izakaya Jūshi and celebrate with everyone there," I suggested, pulling off my boots. I hung my coat in its usual spot and wheeled my bag off to the side. I'd deal with unpacking later. There was something too depressing about packing a bag for a three-day trip and only using it for a few hours.

"No no no. I've had two hours on the road to think of new plans and we will make them happen. Why don't you get cleaned up in the bathroom and slip into something more comfortable? Then you can come join me at the table."

The twinkle in his eye told me he planned to make the night count, and I'd be very happy to follow his guidance. I only needed to play along.

As I made my way to the bedroom, he grabbed his remote and turned on classic 40s jazz music. I changed into yoga pants, a loose top, and my favorite sweater, washed my hands and face in the bathroom, and joined him at the table. Much to my surprise, in the ten minutes I was busy, he had pulled together a wooden board of cheese, olives, cured meats, and crackers. Champagne bubbled away in two flutes on the table, and the bottles of saké I purchased when I was out with Nahoko sat off to the side.

"Wow. What have we here?" I slipped into the chair across from him, admiring his quick handiwork.

"This is what we should have been doing hours ago." He plated a little of each offering and placed it in front of me. "We won't have the five star service nor the hot springs, but with some music playing and champagne, it'll feel just about the same."

He raised his glass, and I followed suit. "To a whole new year in which to make fewer mistakes."

I laughed and touched my glass to his. "Fewer mistakes. And absent friends."

We talked and laughed for over an hour, enjoying the champagne, the food, the music. He relived his day in the kitchen with Hiromi and Andrew, and I tried to find all the funny parts of my day with Nahoko to regale him with. It was hard though, and I struggled to keep a happy face as we approached midnight, until I remembered the woman who was lost on the street.

"I'm so glad you got her back to her family." He reached across the table and squeezed my hand. "You did the right thing."

"You know what, if today taught me anything, it's that family is the most important thing in the world. If things go wrong in a family, people can end up broken and bitter like Nahoko or lost on the street like that poor woman. Nahoko had expectations for how she wanted to be treated by her family, and they didn't meet them."

"It's possible they didn't know how bad things were," he said, coming to Hiromi and Andrew's defense.

"I'm sure of that. She probably never even told them she needed more attention, just expected it." I sighed as I sipped the last of my champagne. "I'm glad we're home. This is where we're needed, you know?" We nodded at each other, sure we'd made the right decision by returning.

Gauging my mood, Yasahiro stood up and offered me his

hand as a slow song came on the radio. I blushed, unable to remember if we had danced together before. I didn't think we had, actually. This would be our first time.

I wrapped my left arm around his waist, and he held my right hand close to his chest. We swayed to the beat, my head on his shoulder, and a sigh upon my lips.

"This is nice. I like dancing with you," I whispered. His head dipped and kissed my neck right below my ear. "Mmmm, I'm glad I'm here with you."

"Me too." He glanced over at the clock and back to me. "I'm going to kiss you when the clock strikes midnight, and then we're going to bed." He raised his eyebrows and I laughed, one of those genuinely happy laughs that comes straight from my stomach.

"And then what?"

"And then we do what we should've done in the first place. We'll start your education in cooking, and we'll spend the day with our families."

The song ended, and the announcer burst onto the radio to herald in a brand-new year. I wrapped my arms around Yasahiro's neck, tipped my face up to his, and started a new phase of our life with a kiss.

CHAPTER
THIRTEEN

When the alarm sounded at 5:00, I woke up in a tangle of legs and arms. We only got about three hours of sleep, but it would have to do until midday when we could nap. Yasahiro ignored the alarm's incessant beeping and snuggled up to me.

"We brought in the new year exactly the way I wanted to," he said, resting his warm hands against my lower back. "And now we're going to begin your education with the knife."

I giggled. "That sounds like the beginning of a horror novel."

He lowered his voice. "She opened the drawer, and the knife burst forth, slashing at random. She had no chance to survive." He hummed creepy music, and I laughed even harder. "Probably too much horror on too little sleep." He rolled away and slammed his hand onto the top of the alarm clock. The bedroom fell into blessed silence.

Today, I would start out the year the way I wanted to continue it, in bed with a loved one, learning something new, and continuing with family.

"Time to get out of bed, Mei," Yasahiro said, swinging his legs over me and sitting up. "We have ozoni soup to make, places to be, and people to see."

The sun was an hour and a half from rising, so we bundled up into sweaters and slippers and turned up the heat. Yasahiro made coffee while I splashed water on my face in the bathroom and combed my hair.

"Okay. You're in charge of the vegetables, and I'll be in charge of the soup." He laid out six carrots, a large bag of shiitake mushrooms, bundles of fresh spinach, a few daikon radishes, and then paused. "What else does your mom put in her soup?"

"Well, toasted mochi, of course, tofu, and yuzu peel."

He opened his refrigerator and retrieved the missing items. He even had yuzu. I don't know why I was surprised by that. He was a chef after all.

"This is going to be great," I said, smiling as I sipped my coffee. "Mom rarely makes her soup until the late morning, after we go to temple. She'll be so excited to see it."

I could do the basic prep on my own, washing and peeling the vegetables and laying them out to be cut. Yasahiro tried to show me how to curl my fingers under so I wouldn't hurt myself chopping vegetables, but I found it uncomfortable and the carrots slid everywhere.

He stared down at my rough cuts, grabbed a fork from the drawer, and handed it to me. "This is what I used as a kid to keep vegetables in place." He speared one end with the fork, and I squealed with glee.

"How come my mom never showed me this?" I asked, as I cut the carrots in even increments. The fork really helped.

"I know your mom. She's the type of person who would rather have you learn something the right way the first time. I'm of the opinion that even if you're doing it wrong, you'll build confidence to do it the right way eventually. I did, and I used the fork for at least ten years."

Somehow I'm not surprised. He was the type to bulldoze through and keep trying until he achieved his goals. He had done the same thing with me.

I hummed as I chopped away. Each item I speared with my fork first, and then, slowly but gaining speed, I made my way through all the vegetables. Yasahiro boiled stock on the stove and toasted mochi rice cakes under the broiler until they puffed up and browned. The smell made my stomach growl, hoping for a meal.

"Wow, is that your stomach?" Yasahiro said with a laugh. "Don't worry. Soup will be ready in no time."

He added the vegetables to the boiling stock, pulling the seaweed out first. "We cook these until tender, then add miso paste and the tofu. The washed spinach goes in last. Always start cooking with the vegetables that take the longest and work your way to the ones that need the least amount of time." I watched as the soup came together, and he turned off the heat. "All done, and look!" He pointed towards the window. The sky had turned from deep obsidian to navy blue. The sun was coming up.

"Mei, you make toast, and I'll brew us up more coffee."

I scrambled past him, popping bread in the toaster and grabbing butter from the fridge. The sky was lightening, bit by bit, and if we didn't hurry, we'd miss it. I've never buttered toast so quickly in all my life.

"I know the perfect place to watch the sun come up," Yasahiro said, pointing up at the ceiling.

"Yes!"

We ran to the door, stumbled over our boots, laughing at each other, drunk on too much coffee and too little sleep. With coats, hats, and scarves on, we left the heated comfort of his apartment.

He grabbed a broom and a blanket from the front hall closet before we ascended the stairs and pushed onto the roof through the few centimeters of snow left up there.

"Ah! We made it just in time. Here, hold my drink." I took his coffee as he made a path for us with the broom, pushed snow from the table, and placed the blanket upon it so we had a place to sit. We ate our toast, munching while steam poured from our lips and the coffee.

"This is cold, but great," I said, resting my head on his shoulder. We both stared at the horizon, watching for the first glimpse of the sun for the new year. There was no better tradition I loved than observing the first sunrise of the year, and to do it with Yasahiro? I couldn't have asked for anything more perfect.

We sipped on our coffee in companionable silence, letting the new rays of the winter sun warm our faces and blind our eyes. I leaned over and kissed him on his cheek.

"Thank you. This is wonderful, and I'd much rather be here with you than in some five-star hotel."

"Me too," he whispered back. He lightly touched my cheek, his fingers skipping down to my chin. "You're my light, Mei. I'd be lost without you."

I smiled, all the words sucked right out of me. My chest was frozen in one long inhale. I could only stare back into his eyes and dart forward to kiss him again. Who needed luck when I had this moment to look back on forever?

When he pulled away, he kissed along my cheek to my ear. "We should finish up inside. I'm an icicle now."

Back inside the apartment, we packaged up the soup to bring to my mom's, but Yasahiro set aside one extra. "For Murata," he said, and I had to stop myself from crying. He had remembered her quicker than I had!

We dropped off a serving of ozoni soup to Murata, my first,

long-term elderly client. She lived around the corner from Yasahiro, and she had been a big help to us during the investigation of Etsuko's murder.

"You didn't have to do this! You must have been up for hours," she said, answering the door in her house coat and slippers.

"We wanted to make sure you had something warm to eat on the first morning of the year," I said, bowing. "And I'll be back in two days to make sure everything's going all right."

The road out to the house was covered with a light dusting of snow, blown onto the pavement overnight. Everything looked to be business as usual at home. Smoke curled from the chimney stack, and several cars were already in the driveway.

"Hello! We're here!" I called out, kicking off my boots in the front hall.

Mom, Chiyo, Goro, and Kumi emerged from the kitchen, Mom's face wide with surprise.

"I thought you were in Hakone!" She opened her arms to hug me, and I gratefully hugged her back.

"We decided it would be better to be at home for New Year's Day. Yasahiro and I even made ozoni soup."

Yasahiro hefted the bags in his arms and passed one off to Goro.

"You helped?" Mom asked, a smile taking over the surprise.

"I did. I chopped vegetables, just like Yasahiro taught me."

"My, my," Mom said, elbowing her best friend, Chiyo, in the ribs. "We may make a chef out of you yet."

Yasahiro laughed. "She can prep, but it'll be awhile before I let her near the stove."

I reached out and pinched his arm as everyone laughed at me. But I laughed too, happy to be home with my family.

"Let's eat soup now, and then we'll all go to the temple for prayers before your brother gets here." Mom gestured for us to sit at the kotatsu. "I'm really proud of you, Mei. And I'm so glad you came back."

"Me too, Mom. I didn't want to be away from family today."

This was the most important place to be.

THANK YOU!

Thank you so much for reading *Ozoni and Onsens*. I hope you enjoyed this little trip away from Chikata.

If you want the next book in the series... *The Daydreamer Detective Opens A Tea Shop* is up next!

Please leave a review of *Ozoni and Onsens* wherever you purchased it. I welcome all reviews positive or negative. Reviews are so important to both authors and readers.

Want news of upcoming books, events, or free stuff? Subscribe to Steph's mailing list at https://www.stephgennaro.com/subscribe/

If you want more books like this one, you can check for more books on my website at http://www.stephgennaro.com/books/

A NOTE FROM STEPH

One of the things I love the most about being an independent author is bringing stories directly to my readers. I only need to dream up my story, write it, edit and proofread it (with outside help), then deliver it to you. How cool is that? It's the wave of the future! Back when I was reading my favorite authors ten years ago, I often thought about how their early careers and the struggles they went through to get the stories they wrote into my hands. I've had friends in publishing for over ten years and hearing what happens behind the scenes always made my head spin. The world has changed for the better.

An author like me would never have found her audience ten years ago. As you can see from my books, I write simple, easy prose. A recent review even called into question whether I was writing for fourth graders or not! (Laughs.) Yes, it's true. I do boil down my work into clean and precise sentences. I write like I talk because I want to talk to you. That's the most important thing for me to remember every time I sit down to get something done. You and me, we're here because we want to be, and that's something to be thankful for.

This little side story came at a time when I needed to learn a little more about Mei, Yasahiro, and their motives for going into the rest of the series. It also solidified how I feel about my writing career. How it's important for me to have fun and enjoy this ride. I should live in the moment, revel in the details and synergy of moments that come together when I least expect it. Writing is magical! And having fun writing is what I want to do in 2017. Like Mei and Yasahiro who have realized family will play an important role in their lives, I have also realized that writing will be an important part of my life from here forward. It's no longer just a dream. It's reality.

Thanks for reading and living my dream with me!

I look forward to bringing you more stories in the future.

A NOTE ABOUT CHANGES TO THIS BOOK

In case you missed it in the Foreword...

In Japanese, the most common way of showing respect to another person's social standing is with the use of honorific suffixes that are appended on the end of either first or last names. The most common, -san, means either Mr., Ms., or Mrs.

In earlier versions of this book, and in the whole series, I did use these honorific suffixes. But for 2019 and onward, I have switched to the English way in order to make this series more accessible to English speakers. I hope you enjoy this version!

The town in this novel, Chikata, is completely fictional, though the area I put it in is not. Saitama prefecture is located to the west of Tokyo, and many of the eastern areas are considered to be suburbs of the city. Chikata is located farther out west, nearer to the prefectures of Nagano and Gunma.

ABOUT THE AUTHOR

Steph Gennaro is a long-time Japanophile, and she's been studying Japanese culture and language for over 20 years. She loves dreaming of far-off places, going for walks with her dog, Lulu Ninja Assassin, hanging out with her family, and reading outside in the summertime. There is no better season than summer. She's a Capricorn, mother, knitter, and web developer, and pasta is her favorite meal. Steph Gennaro is her pen name for cozy mysteries, but she also writes science fiction romance and many other genres.

Find her online at...
www.stephgennaro.com

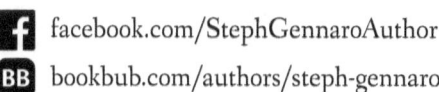

facebook.com/StephGennaroAuthor

bookbub.com/authors/steph-gennaro

www.ingramcontent.com/pod-product-compliance
Lightning Source LLC
Chambersburg PA
CBHW032110170626
46808CB00008B/3003